DISNEY PRINCESS

Belle's Friendship Invention

By Amy Sky Koster

Illustrated by Alan Batson and Jean-Paul Orpinas

A Random House PICTUREBACK® Book

Random House 🏠 New York

Copyright © 2016 Disney Enterprises, Inc. All rights reserved. Published in the United States by
Random House Children's Books, a division of Penguin Random House LLC, 1745 Broadway,
New York, NY 10019, and in Canada by Penguin Random House Canada Limited, Toronto,
in conjunction with Disney Enterprises, Inc. Pictureback, Random House, and the Random House
colophon are registered trademarks of Penguin Random House LLC.
randomhousekids.com
ISBN 978-0-7364-3735-6
Printed in the United States of America
10 9 8 7 6 5 4 3 2

*B*elle was too excited to read! Today the first annual Invention Convention was in town, and she was attending with her father, Maurice.

While Maurice was setting up, Belle explored. She
had never seen the town square so full of activity!

Everywhere Belle looked,
she saw amazing inventions.

Some had lots of

bells and whistles...

... while others were quite practical.

Some were simple and sweet.

Just when Belle thought she'd seen it all, she noticed a crowd near one corner of the square. She squeezed through to see what everyone was oohing and aahing over.

"There must be something exciting in . . ."

". . . here," Belle whispered. She was nearly speechless when she finally made her way to the center of the circle.

There stood the first-place invention and its inventor—a girl Belle's age!

The girl was just about to demonstrate how her invention worked and was looking for a volunteer. Belle raised her hand.

The inventor selected Belle. "I'm Simone," she said.
"What's your name?"

"I'm Belle."

"Hello, Belle. Now, would you please place a handful
of leaves right here?" Simone pointed to her invention.

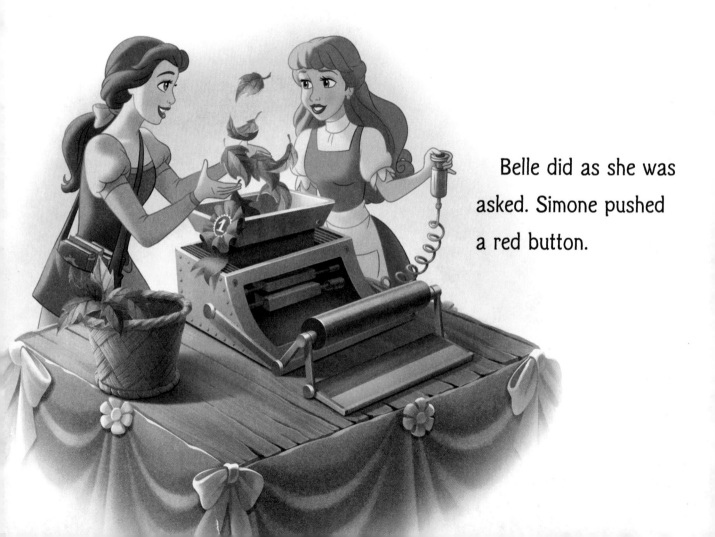

Belle did as she was
asked. Simone pushed
a red button.

The machine started to whir, and then one smooth piece of paper popped out.

"Et voilà!" cried Simone.

Her invention pressed leaves into paper!

Suddenly, the machine made a strange sound
and started spitting pieces of paper everywhere.

The machine finally stopped when it had run out of leaves.

Simone was embarrassed. "What am I going to do with all this paper?" she asked.

Belle had gathered all the papers into a neat pile. "Write on them, of course!" she exclaimed.

The two girls sat down beneath a tree.

"Let's write a message that will make someone smile," said Belle.

"That's an excellent idea," said Simone.

They wrote a special note and delivered it to the florist.

"This is fun!" said Simone.

"Let's write another one."

Belle and Simone delivered their next note to the bookseller. They hid outside and watched him read it.

The girls delivered their last note to Maurice.

This time, they didn't hide.
Maurice read the note aloud:
"'Smile! You are loved.'"

At the end of the day, the convention was over. Belle helped Simone pack up her invention.

She would miss her new friend.

But when Belle opened her book that evening, she was sure their friendship would last.

"That was amazing!" Charlotte said when the show had ended. "But the way your mama told the story when we were little girls is still my favorite."

Tiana knew she and Charlotte would always agree on what mattered most:

being best friends forever!

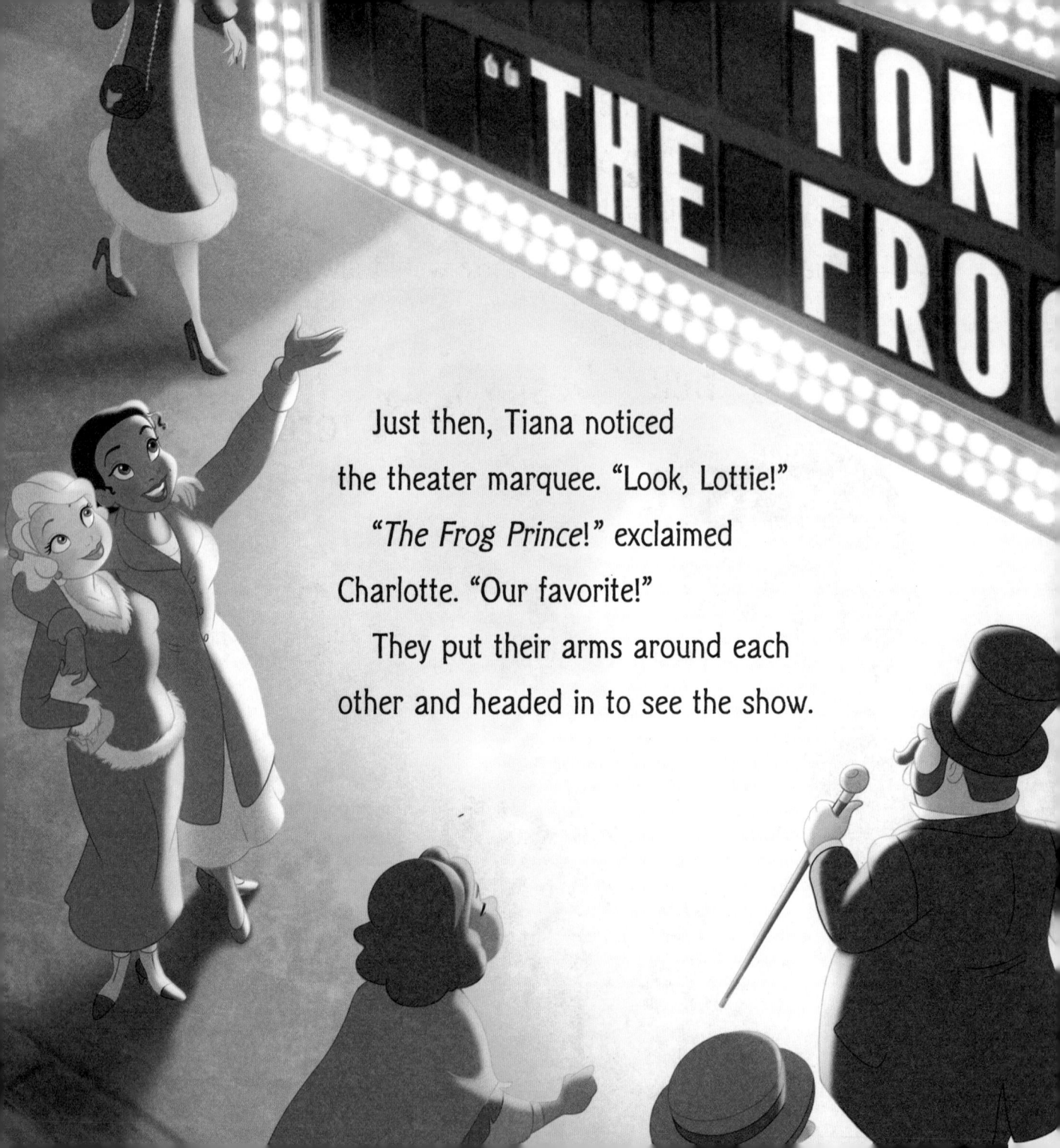

Just then, Tiana noticed
the theater marquee. "Look, Lottie!"

"*The Frog Prince!*" exclaimed
Charlotte. "Our favorite!"

They put their arms around each
other and headed in to see the show.

The friends hugged.

"I'm sorry!" Charlotte cried.

"Me too!" Tiana said. "I want to spend time with you, Lottie, but maybe shopping and cooking aren't the best ways to do that."

"I agree!" said Charlotte. "So what can we do?"

That night, Charlotte and Tiana knew
they had to find each other. Tiana
spotted Charlotte in front of the theater.

THEATER

TONIGHT
"THE FROG PRINCE"

She missed her
best friend, too.

Meanwhile, Tiana grimaced.

She grumbled.

Most of all, she missed her best friend.

When Charlotte got home, she complained.

She fussed.

. . . *WHOOOOSH!* It went up in flames!

Tiana came in just as the smoke cleared.

"Oh, Lottie!" she exclaimed. "What did you do?"

Charlotte didn't know what had happened.

She started to cry.

Charlotte did a great job!

"Can you handle making the rest?" asked Tiana.

"Is my daddy's name Big Daddy?" replied Charlotte. "Of course I can!"

After Tiana left, Charlotte heated up a vat of oil. When it was ready, she dropped the dough in, and . . .

"I'll help you at the restaurant!" she announced. "Won't that be fun?"
Tiana wasn't so sure, but she wanted to at least give it a try.
She showed Charlotte how to make beignets in fun shapes.

Tiana and Charlotte both felt
bad that they had disappointed
each other during their
shopping trip. The next day,
they apologized.

"I'm glad that's over," said
Charlotte, "because I have
another brilliant idea about
how we can spend time
together!"

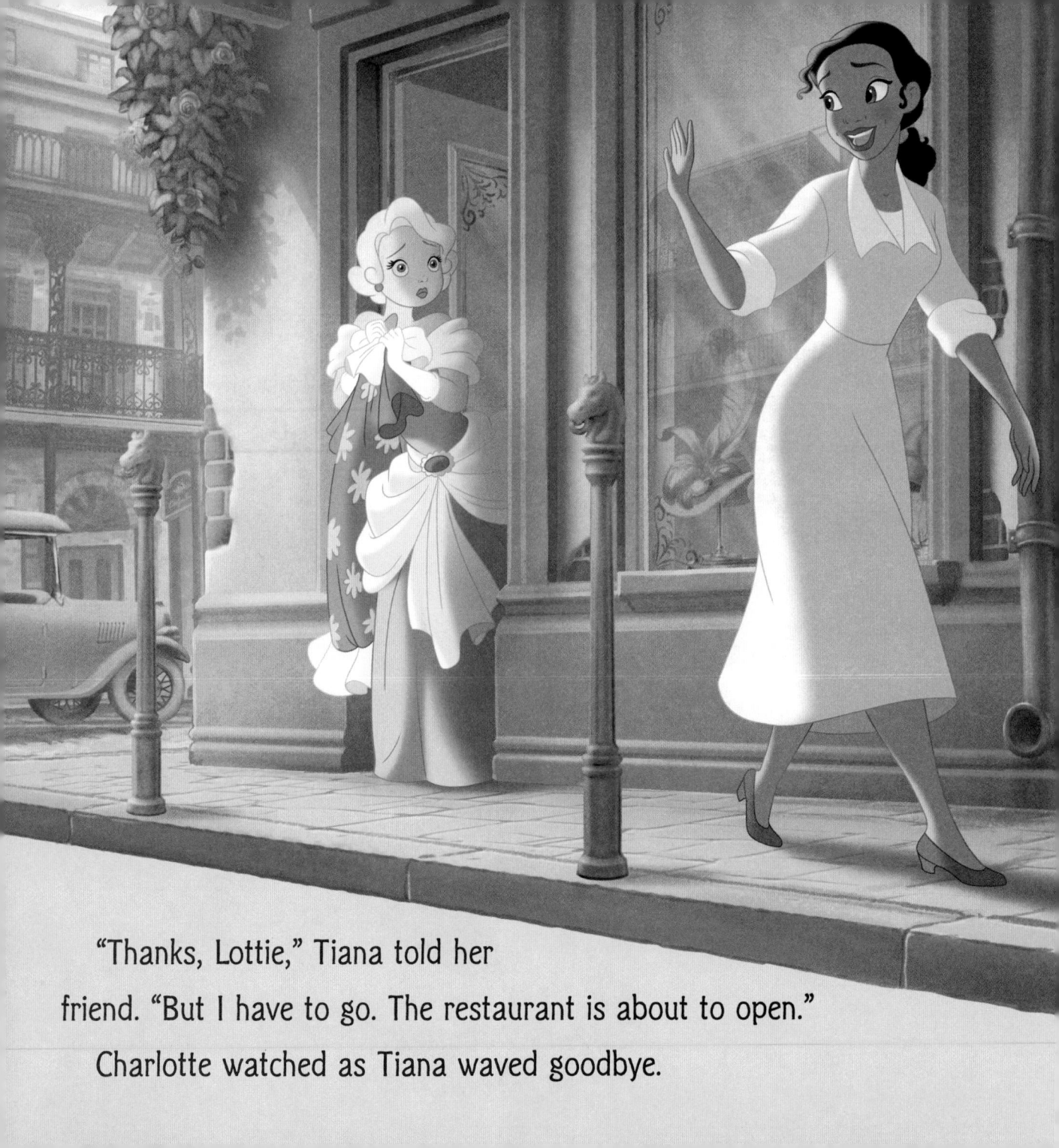

"Thanks, Lottie," Tiana told her
friend. "But I have to go. The restaurant is about to open."
Charlotte watched as Tiana waved goodbye.

"I love them, too," Charlotte said. "But there's always room for a new dress. How about this one?"

"But, Lottie . . ."

"Or this one?" continued Charlotte, holding up another dress.

"Me?" Tiana answered. "But I love the dresses Mama made for me. I don't need another."

"...and this one ..."

"...and this one!"

"Almost done?" Tiana asked.

"Just one more thing," said Charlotte. "We need a dress for you!"

But Charlotte wasn't so sure.
She wanted to try on everything.
Hours later, she finally started
to make her choices.
"I'll take this one . . ."

Charlotte took Tiana to the Bayou
Boutique and tried on a poufy dress.
"Isn't this darling?" asked Charlotte.
"It's swell, Lottie," replied Tiana.
"Shall we get it and go?"

Charlotte pouted. "You're always so busy with your restaurant and Naveen. I just want to spend time with you."

Charlotte had a point. Tiana had been very busy.

"All right," Tiana agreed. "We can go shopping." She plugged her ears while Charlotte squealed with delight.

Tiana sighed. "I hardly
have time to sit, let alone shop, Lottie."

One afternoon, Princess Tiana was visiting her best friend, Charlotte. "I have nothing to wear, Tia," said Charlotte as she rummaged through her closet. "We have to go shopping."

Tiana's Friendship Fix-Up

By Cynthea Liu

Illustrated by Alan Batson and Adrienne Brown

A Random House PICTUREBACK® Book

Random House New York

Copyright © 2016 Disney Enterprises, Inc. All rights reserved. Published in the United States by Random House Children's Books, a division of Penguin Random House LLC, 1745 Broadway, New York, NY 10019, and in Canada by Penguin Random House Canada Limited, Toronto, in conjunction with Disney Enterprises, Inc. Pictureback, Random House, and the Random House colophon are registered trademarks of Penguin Random House LLC.
randomhousekids.com
ISBN 978-0-7364-3735-6
Printed in the United States of America
10 9 8 7 6 5 4 3 2